Streamline Graded Readers
Level 3

African Adventure

Margaret Iggulden

Series Editors:
Bernard Hartley and Peter Viney

GW00726169

OXFORD UNIVERSITY PRESS

Oxford University Press
Walton Street, Oxford OX2 6DP

Oxford New York Toronto
Delhi Bombay Calcutta Madras Karachi
Petaling Jaya Singapore Hong Kong Tokyo
Nairobi Dar es Salaam Cape Town
Melbourne Auckland

and associated companies in
Berlin Ibadan

OXFORD and OXFORD ENGLISH are trade marks
of Oxford University Press

ISBN 0 19 421911 9

© Oxford University Press 1988

First published 1988
Fifth impression 1990

Illustrated by: Chris Molan
Cover illustration: Jane Smith

Printed in Hong Kong

Teresa looked out of the window of the plane and saw the
lights of London below her. 'I can't believe it. I'm really going
to Kenya. Goodbye, cold England, I'm going to the sun! Six
months in Africa. I'm so excited.'

'Are you going to Kenya for a holiday?' asked the woman
next to her.

'No. I'm going to work at a special hospital in Nairobi. I'm
going to work with an American doctor for several months.'

3

'That's very interesting.'

'Yes, he's a friend of my father's. His name is Dr McCall. He's very clever,' said Teresa.

'Dr McCall? I've read about his work in the newspaper. He's famous. Doesn't he study flowers and trees?' The woman looked interested.

'I'm not sure.' Teresa laughed. 'I'm working with him because I can speak Nandi, one of the Kenyan languages. I was born in Kenya. We returned to England when I was three. But my father always speaks Nandi to me. He loves Africa. He was born just outside Nairobi and lived there for thirty years. He loves the people and the country. I think he can speak five African languages.'

'What's his name?'

'Dunn. Thomas Dunn. And I'm Teresa Dunn.'

'*Chamgei*, Teresa. My name's Anna Holmes.'

'You speak Nandi, too! *Mising*, Anna!'

They both smiled.

'Where do you live, Anna?' asked Teresa.

'I live in the west,' said Anna. 'I'll give you my address. Come and visit me.'

'Thank you. Do you often do this in Africa?'

'What?'

'Invite strangers to stay with you?'

'Oh yes. A lot of people will invite you to their homes.'

'In Europe people don't do that.'

'No. Africa is quite different. Don't you remember?'

'No, I only remember the hot sun.'

Anna looked at her and smiled. 'I think you'll learn a lot in Kenya. Now I need some sleep.' She shut her eyes.

Teresa felt happy. She had a new friend already. What a nice woman! She looked at Anna. Her hair was white, and there were a lot of lines on her face, but she looked strong. Teresa thought about the next few months. 'Life is exciting. Will I be able to travel around the country? Will I be able to see wild animals? Will it be dangerous? Will . . . ?' She fell asleep.

The next day Teresa went to the hospital. It was ten o'clock and it was already very hot. She found Dr McCall's office on the second floor.

'Teresa? Hi! Welcome to Kenya.' A short, fat man with black hair and dark glasses stood up. 'Come and sit down. You look hot. This is the hottest time of the year. Would you like a drink of water? Or a cup of tea?'

'Could I have some water, please?' said Teresa.

She looked round the room. There were a lot of photographs on the walls. They were all of Dr McCall. One showed him with a gun. He was standing beside a dead animal. Another showed him with a group of Africans. Why did he have so many photographs of himself? What kind of man was he?

'Don't forget. You must drink a lot of water here, or you'll become ill. Be careful, wash all fruit before you eat it. What else must I tell you?' The doctor sat back in his chair and put his hands together. 'Always wear a hat when you go out in the sun. I don't want you to be ill.'

Teresa felt that she was back at school. 'Must, must not, be careful, do this, don't do that . . . Was it a mistake to come here and work for Dr McCall?' she thought.

The doctor suddenly smiled. 'I'm sure we'll work well together, Teresa. Your father and I are very good friends. I want to look after you. Sometimes Africa is a difficult country. Beautiful, interesting, but also dangerous.'

Now she understood. He was just worried about her. But she was eighteen and she was old enough to look after herself. And she had read her father's books about Kenya. She knew a lot.

'Tell me about your work, Dr McCall.'

He went to the door and looked outside. Then he locked it. 'Now, I'm going to tell you a secret. No one here in the hospital knows anything about it.'

'No one?' Teresa nearly laughed. This was just like a James Bond story.

He spoke quietly. 'I've discovered a medicine woman near Lake Victoria who can prevent a terrible sickness. No one else knows about her. Only me.'

'What is the sickness?' Teresa asked.

'It's river blindness. Many Africans catch it when they are babies. Slowly . . . very slowly they go blind. There are hundreds and thousands of men, women and children with the sickness. Think about it . . . Thousands of people cannot see.'

'How do they catch it?' Teresa felt sad. It sounded terrible.

'A little fly that lives in rivers bites people. The fly leaves an egg in the bite, and this becomes a tiny worm. This worm gets into the blood and moves through the body . . . to the feet, legs, head, everywhere. It attacks the eyes and, very slowly, the person goes blind. The eyes become red and tired, and under a microscope you can see silver lines in them. The lines are the sign of river blindness.'

Teresa felt terrible. This wasn't in the books she read. 'How do the people live?'

'In many villages, nearly everyone is blind. The young children can see. They have to hold the hands of the blind people.'

'Do they work?' said Teresa.

'They have to. The children take them to the river or the forest. They bring water or find wood for the fire.'

'That's a very difficult life.'

'Yes, but they help each other. It's more difficult for us. When you live in a city, people don't help each other.'

Dr McCall took off his glasses. His eyes looked strange, Teresa thought. What was the matter with him? 'Can this medicine woman near Lake Victoria cure these blind people?' she asked.

'No. She can't cure them. When someone has river blindness, no doctor or medicine woman can cure it. That's impossible.'

'But what does she do?' asked Teresa.

'She's found a special flower. She gives it to the young people. Then they don't get river blindness.'

Teresa was excited. 'That's wonderful! . . . But what is my job, doctor?' she asked.

'I can't speak Nandi and you can. I want you to come with me to the forest. You must talk to this medicine woman for me.'

'But why me? Why don't you use a Kenyan?' asked Teresa.

'Because I want it to be a secret. And you don't know anyone here.'

7

Teresa wanted to ask a lot more questions, but the doctor started to get up.

'OK. We'll leave on Monday. Bring enough clothes for a few days. Buy a hat . . . and a water-bottle. I'll bring everything else. Now, goodbye, and I'll see you at eight o'clock on Monday. I must see someone from F.D.I. now.'

'F.D.I.?' said Teresa. She stood up and moved towards the door.

'It's an American drug company. They're also interested in medicines for river blindness.' He shook his finger at her. 'Now, remember, it's a secret. Don't talk to anyone about it.'

○ ○ ○ ○

Teresa had lunch in a restaurant in the middle of Nairobi. It was very busy and nearly all the tables were full. She sat and thought about river blindness, the medicine woman . . . and Dr McCall. 'Why must it be a secret?' she thought.

'Is this seat free?' She looked up. A tall Kenyan was standing beside her.

'Oh yes. Please . . . sit down.'

'Coffee, please,' the young man said to the waiter. 'A very strong one. Perhaps it will wake me up. I'm very tired.' He smiled at Teresa. He had a very friendly smile, Teresa thought. She smiled back at him.

'Have you been working hard?' she asked.

'Yes, I'm a reporter. I was working until three o'clock last night. I was writing about that Chinese man. You know, a lion killed him yesterday.'

'A lion?'

'Yes, it happened in one of the parks. It attacked him and bit him very badly. The man lost a lot of blood and he died last night.'

Teresa pushed her hamburger away. 'I don't think I'm hungry now.'

He laughed. 'Usually I write more interesting stories.'

'What kind of stories?'

'Oh, about bad people that try to get lots of money.'

'How?'

'Well, some people kill animals for money. There are a lot of them in Kenya.' He drank some coffee. 'What are you doing here? Are you on holiday?'

Teresa knew she had to be careful. She told him about the doctor, but she did not tell him about the medicine woman, the flower and the river blindness.

'Dr McCall?' he said. 'I know him. He's a clever man. He does a lot of work on African diseases, doesn't he? But he won't talk about his work. He won't tell anyone.'

Teresa kept quiet.

'Some people say he's working on something very secret.'

'Really? I don't know anything about it.' Teresa tried to look surprised.

'Don't you? Well, keep your eyes and ears open. When you have a story, telephone me. I know he's working on something.' He took out a card.

Teresa read:

> *Christopher Mwale*
> *Reporter*
> *The African Telegraph*
> *P.O. Box 471*
> *Nairobi*
> *Tel 8195226*

'Well, I must go.' He finished his coffee and stood up. 'Don't work too hard for the old man. Goodbye now.' He smiled at her and left the restaurant.

Teresa looked down at his chair. She saw a copy of his newspaper, *The African Telegraph*. She picked it up and looked at it. She saw the words 'river blindness' and began to read.

The African Telegraph

RIVER BLINDNESS:
THE FIGHT TO STOP IT

Many people believe that there will soon be a medicine for river blindness. This medicine will not cure the disease, but it will prevent it. Doctors at *Village International*, the famous charity in Nairobi, are testing many different medicines and say they will find the right one soon. And they are very excited because they have just had some good news from Norway. Dr Ndeti, the director of Village International, said today:

'Norway has promised Village International three million dollars when we find a medicine for river blindness. With this money we can give the medicine free to every child in every village in Kenya. Nobody in Kenya will go blind from river blindness again. But we must find the right medicine quickly. If we don't find it, Norway will give the money to another charity.'

But F.D.I., the American drug company, are also looking for medicines for river blindness. They have promised one million dollars to the person who finds the right medicine. Dr Ndeti says, 'F.D.I. will make the medicine and sell it to all African countries. But the poor people in our villages cannot buy expensive American medicines.'

Teresa threw down the newspaper. 'Money!' she thought. 'Is this why Dr McCall wants the medicine woman and her flower to be a secret? Maybe he wants to sell the medicine to F.D.I. and become rich. That's terrible. He's a doctor. He should want to help people. Why doesn't he *give* the secret to Village International? Then Norway will give them all that money . . .' Suddenly she remembered. 'This morning! Dr McCall was meeting someone from F.D.I. That's it! I think he wants to get the million dollars for himself. But what can I do? How can I stop him? He's my father's friend . . . Maybe I'm wrong. I don't know enough about it.'

◀ ◀ ▶ ▶

On Monday morning Dr McCall, Teresa and Obediah the driver drove towards Lake Victoria on good roads. Teresa loved the wide sky, the high valleys, the little villages. This was Africa! The hills looked blue and far away. The country was green and beautiful. Brightly coloured birds flew everywhere. Women were walking along the road. They were carrying heavy bundles of wood on their backs. Children were carrying water in large pots on their heads.

'Why aren't the children in school?' Teresa wanted to know.

'They must help their families,' said the doctor.

'And where are the men?'

'They're talking with their friends,' said Obediah. 'In Africa the women do the work.'

'That's terrible,' said Teresa.

Dr McCall laughed. 'Why did he laugh?' thought Teresa angrily. It wasn't funny.

At about five o'clock they arrived in the Nandi area. They stopped near a village. Dr McCall walked down to a small lake and sat down on a rock. He watched the birds. Teresa helped Obediah. They put up the tents and cooked some food. Teresa was feeling very tired and hungry. She was also angry with the doctor. 'Why doesn't he help us?' she thought. 'I don't like him. He doesn't want to help anybody.'

Just then, Teresa saw a line of people. They were walking towards the village. There were five women, and in front she could see a little boy. He was holding the stick of the first woman. The next held onto her. Teresa called out to them. They heard her, and called back, but they did not look at her. They walked slowly past the three tents. Teresa could see their eyes. All the women were blind.

Teresa felt very sad. 'I will do anything to help these people,' she thought. 'Anything.'

The next day they all got up at four o'clock. The medicine woman lived several kilometres away in the forest. There were no roads, and they had to walk. 'It'll be a long, hot walk,' thought Teresa. 'I'm going to have a swim.' She ran down to the lake.

'Stop!' shouted Dr McCall. 'Don't touch the water!'

'What is it now? It's always "don't do this" and "don't do that",' thought Teresa. She walked back to the tents.

'You'll get sick from that water. It's still,' said the doctor. 'I told you yesterday. In Africa you mustn't swim in still water. You'll catch a disease. In a few years you'll get sick and you'll feel very tired. That's why many of the people in this area can't work very hard.'

'I forgot,' said Teresa, angry at herself.

'Wash in the water that I brought,' said the doctor. He sounded tired. 'And listen to my advice, please. I've lived in this country all my life. I know it better than you.'

Teresa ate her breakfast silently. 'I don't like him,' she thought. 'And he doesn't like me either. He thinks I'm silly. Well . . . I'm not.'

After breakfast Dr McCall told Teresa to get ready. She put on some strong shoes. She also put on her new hat and filled her water-bottle. 'I'm learning how to live in Africa,' she said to Dr McCall. He smiled, but said nothing.

They walked for several hours. The trees were very tall, with huge, bright green leaves. Teresa could not see the sky. Birds screamed high above them. It was very hot, and the air was still, and heavy. There was no wind. Teresa felt she could not breathe.

They saw nobody for hours, but then, suddenly, there was a village in front of them.

'Stop here for a minute, Teresa.'

She sat down immediately and drank all the water from her bottle. She was very hot, and her legs ached.

'Don't drink too much too quickly,' said the doctor.

'Yes, yes. I know.'

13

'Now, the medicine woman lives in this village. Her name is Rose. I want you to talk to her. Ask her to show you the flower . . . the flower that prevents river blindness.'

'But I thought you knew the flower?' Teresa was surprised.

'No, she won't tell me. But you are a woman, and you can speak Nandi. She will like that. And she can have money. Tell her. She can have as much money as she wants.'

Teresa felt unhappy. Why was he talking about money? 'But who is going to give her this money?' she asked.

'That doesn't matter. Don't ask so many questions. But she must show you the flower. I have to know . . . I . . .' He stopped. 'Come on. Let's go.'

Teresa did not like this. It didn't feel right. What money was he talking about? She wanted to ask him about Village International and F.D.I. But she was afraid. He was beginning to look angry.

They walked into the village. There were several huts and a lot of little children were playing outside them. They ran up to Teresa and tried to touch her long hair. She laughed and asked them their names.

'There's Rose,' said the doctor, and pointed to an old woman standing by the door of a hut. 'Come on. Don't talk to those children. We have to work.'

Teresa walked over to Rose, and spoke to her in Nandi. '*Chamgei*, Rose,' she said.

The old woman looked surprised, then pleased. '*Mising*,' she replied. She began to ask Teresa questions, and soon they were talking quickly. Teresa told her she was from England, and Rose's old face smiled. 'Good, good,' she said.

'What are you talking about?' Dr McCall asked.

'I'm asking her about her family and telling her about mine.'

'Well, hurry up. We haven't got all day.'

Teresa told Rose that she was very sad because there were so many blind people in Kenya. She wanted to help them.

'But I help them,' said Rose. 'Every day I go to the forest and cut some flowers. From these flowers I make the medicine. All

14

the young people in my village can see. No one goes blind
here.'

'Which flower do you use, Rose?'

'Why do you want to know? It's a secret.'

'Tell me, Rose. Then I can go to Nairobi and tell all the
doctors there. You can help many people in Kenya, and in
Africa.'

Rose shook her head slowly. 'I don't know . . . I don't know,'
she said.

'What's the matter?' asked Dr McCall.

'Nothing. She's thinking.'

Rose looked around the village. Her eyes were red and tired.
'Rose will go blind,' Teresa thought.

'Yes, I will go blind soon,' said the old woman.

Teresa looked at her sadly. 'Rose, will you tell me the secret?
Tell me about the flower you use. Then the doctors can make
the medicine from the flowers. They can help many people in
Kenya . . . in all Africa . . . Please, Rose.'

Rose looked at Teresa. 'You are a good girl. But . . .' She
looked at the doctor. 'He was here before, with another man.'
She shook her head again. 'I don't know.'

'Tell her she can have money,' said Dr McCall.

'Rose . . .' Teresa began. What could she say? 'The doctor
wants to help. He will give you money . . .'

'No! I don't want money! I will not tell him. I do not trust
him. I will tell you. Only you. Go to Nairobi and find the good
people. Tell them.'

'But . . .' Teresa was worried. 'What will he do to me?' she
thought.

'I will tell you . . . or nobody.'

Teresa turned to Dr McCall. She looked down at her hands.
'Well?' he asked.

'She will tell me. But she won't tell you. She doesn't . . .
er . . . I must tell the doctors when I get to Nairobi.'

Dr McCall's face was red. 'What? What?' he shouted.

'I'm sorry. That's what she said.'

'You're lying,' Dr McCall said angrily. 'You don't really want to help these people. Have you asked her . . .'

'I'm not lying,' Teresa shouted. 'And I do want to help them.'

Rose came and stood beside Teresa. She spoke quietly to her. 'He must go away now. You can stay here for a few hours. I will show you the flower. Harriet, one of my grandchildren, will take you back to your camp later.'

Teresa turned to Dr McCall. 'She wants you to go back to the camp, Dr McCall.'

'And you? What are you going to do?'

'Rose wants me to stay here for a few hours. I'll come back later with her granddaughter.'

'OK, OK. You talk to Rose. I'll wait for you at the camp.' The doctor walked away into the forest.

'Now let's go and see the flowers,' said Rose.

○ ○ ○ ○

Teresa followed Rose and Harriet into the forest. It was very dark under the trees, and very hot. Teresa felt thirsty, but her water-bottle was empty. They walked for half an hour, then they crossed a river. Rose went to some tall trees beside the river. She cut off some leaves and showed them to Teresa. 'This is it,' she said.

'I thought it was a flower.'

'I wanted to keep my secret. Look at the tree. Look carefully. You must remember it.'

Teresa looked carefully. The tree was tall and had small, yellow-green leaves.

'Look at the leaves,' Rose said.

Teresa saw there were yellow lines on the leaves. She must not forget them.

'Take some. Now, let's make a fire and we will boil the leaves three times.'

Teresa found some wood and they made a small fire. Rose took a pot from under some sticks. Harriet went to the river

and got a little water. Then she put the pot on the fire and threw the leaves in. 'Is that all?' Teresa asked Rose.

'We must boil the leaves three times,' said Rose. 'Then we wait for an hour. When it's cold, you can use it.'

'That's easy.' Teresa laughed.

'I did not say it was difficult. But now it is your secret . . . and mine. Use it well. Show the leaves only to the good people. Now Harriet will take you back to your camp.'

o o o o

Teresa arrived back at the camp late in the afternoon. The young English girl was very tired, very hot, and very thirsty. Her eyes were burning and her head ached. 'What am I going to say to Dr McCall?' she thought. 'And what is he going to say to me?' It was difficult to think clearly.

'Hello, Teresa. I know you are hot and thirsty,' said Dr McCall. He came up to her and took her arm. 'You must rest.' His voice was kind.

Teresa was surprised. Maybe everything was all right. Maybe she was wrong about the doctor.

'I've made you some special Kenyan tea. You'll feel better soon.' He looked at her carefully. 'Did Rose . . . No . . . You must rest first.'

Teresa sat down and drank the tea quickly. 'Thanks very much, doctor.'

She began to feel very sleepy. Something strange was happening. Her head felt very light. She felt sick. She couldn't move her hands or feet. 'Was Dr McCall . . . ? Rose didn't trust him. I don't trust him. Why did he give me the tea? Was there something in it?' His face came towards her.

'Feeling tired, Teresa? Are you hot? Is your head feeling strange?'

'Questions, questions,' thought Teresa. 'Leave me alone,' she said. 'I want to sleep.' She pushed him away. 'What was in that tea? What did you put in it? What is happening to me? You're going to sell the secret . . .'

But Teresa was asleep. She was dreaming about a huge wild animal. It was coming closer and closer. It wanted to eat her. It was green with yellow lines. She was near a river. The animal was going to catch her. She was on a fire. She was very hot. 'Are you going to boil me three times?' she shouted in her dream. 'Yes, three times,' said the animal. It had red eyes. Then the animal went away. She was cold.

❍ ❍ ❍ ❍

Teresa woke up in her tent. She felt sick. 'What happened?' she thought. Maybe she needed some water. She felt very hot. 'Dr McCall!' she shouted. There was no answer. She opened her tent and looked outside. The tents were there, but there was no car, no Dr McCall and no Obediah. 'Where are they?' she thought. 'Have they left me here alone?'

'Miss Teresa!'

Teresa jumped. Harriet, Rose's granddaughter, was standing in front of her.

'Miss Teresa. I saw you were sick. I stayed behind your tent. The white man asked you questions, and you told him the secret. You told him about the leaves. Then they went away in the car.' The little girl looked up at Teresa. She was crying.

'Oh no! The tea . . . I remember. It was the tea! I think he put something in the tea. I talked because of the tea.' Teresa was very angry, with Dr McCall, with herself, with everybody.

'What can I do? I must get to Nairobi before the doctor. He will sell the secret to F.D.I. I'm sure that's what he'll do. They'll give him lots of money. He's a bad man, I'm sure. I must find that reporter, Christopher Mwale. He will help me. I must see Village International and tell them. I have to get to Nairobi . . . quickly!' She held her head in her hands. 'Oh, my head aches.'

Harriet looked at her with big, round eyes. 'I will take you to the big house. They will help you.'

'How far is it?'

'Two hours' walk. But Miss Teresa, you look sick. You

must drink lots of water.'

'There isn't time. I must get to Nairobi. Let's go!'

They walked quickly through the forest. Teresa wanted to lie down and sleep. Everything ached. Her legs, her head, her eyes. But she walked and walked and thought of the doctor. 'I must stop him . . . I must stop him.'

They left the forest and came to a narrow road. It was beginning to get dark. Harriet stopped. 'Walk along here for twenty minutes and you will see the house. An English woman lives there. She will help you. Goodbye, Miss Teresa.'

'Goodbye, Harriet, and thank you.'

Teresa ran, then walked along the road. Her head felt strange and her eyes were burning again. Suddenly she came to a big house with a large garden. A white-haired woman was sitting in a chair outside the door.

'Hello!' called Teresa. 'Please help me. I'm in trouble.'

The woman stood up. It was Anna Holmes. 'Well, it's Teresa Dunn! What are you doing here? What's the matter? You look hot and dirty. Have you been discovering Africa?'

'Anna! Oh Anna, I'm glad to see you. Please help me. I must get to Nairobi immediately.'

'Sit down, Teresa. Would you like some water? You look . . .'

'Anna. This is important. I've learnt a secret. This secret, well . . . it can prevent river blindness.'

'What? Are you sure?'

'Yes, of course I'm sure. But I must get to Nairobi . . . I must tell . . .' Teresa suddenly felt very tired and sick.

'Why don't you go tomorrow? You look terrible. I'll get you some water. Sit down and rest.'

'No, I must go now. Listen.' Teresa tried to speak clearly. 'Dr McCall is going to sell the secret to an American drug company. They'll give him one million dollars for it. They'll make the medicine and the people here won't have enough money to buy it. He's only interested in himself. I'm sure he's working for this company. He's a bad man. I don't trust him.'

Then Teresa told Anna everything – about Village International, about Rose and Harriet, about Dr McCall's strange tea, about her terrifying dream. 'And Harriet heard me. I told him the secret while I was sleeping.'

Anna jumped up. 'OK. Don't worry. I'll telephone the Flying Doctor now.'

Teresa lay on the ground. 'Will I get to Nairobi in time?' she thought.

Anna came back quickly. 'The doctor will be here in thirty minutes. She'll take you to Nairobi in her plane. Then you can tell your secret to everyone.'

Teresa sat up. 'That's wonderful! Thank you, Anna. But what is the Flying Doctor?'

'It's a charity. When a person is sick and there's no hospital near them, the doctor flies in, picks up the sick person, and takes them to Nairobi. They've saved many lives. Now, drink this water . . .'

Two hours later Teresa was in Nairobi. She was sitting in Christopher Mwale's office. She told him everything. His eyes shone. This was a big story.

'You're sure he wants to sell this secret to F.D.I.?'

'I'm sure,' Teresa said. 'I read all about it in *The African Telegraph*. He'll get a million dollars from F.D.I. and Village International won't get the money from Norway. Then they won't be able to give the medicine to every child in Kenya. And F.D.I. will make the medicine, but the poor people won't be able to buy it. Why don't you know all this? It was in *your* newspaper.'

'Well,' said Christopher, 'I didn't know about Dr McCall and Rose, did I? OK. I'll write this story and then we'll go and see Village International.'

'No. Let's go and see them now. I'm afraid. Dr McCall may be at F.D.I. already.'

'OK,' said Christopher. 'That'll make a better story.'

'Is that all you're worried about – your story? What about all the blind people in your country?' Teresa was getting very angry.

'All right. Let's go now.'

'Dr McCall only wants to be rich. And you only want to get good stories for your newspaper. Who's worrying about the Africans? I'm tired of you both.'

'Teresa. It's OK. Let's go.'

◆ ◆ ◆ ◆

Teresa and Christopher ran into the Village International building. A woman was talking on a telephone. Teresa went over to her. 'Excuse me, but this is very important. I must speak to the director of Village International. I must see him now.'

The woman was surprised. 'Dr Ndeti? He's very busy at the moment. His office is next door. I'll ask . . .'

But Teresa was already at the door. She opened it and walked in. Christopher followed her.

'Hey! You can't just go in . . .' the woman called.

There were a lot of people in the director's office. They all looked up when Teresa and Christopher walked in. Teresa spoke to a large Kenyan man sitting at the top of the table.

'Excuse me, are you Dr Ndeti? I'm sorry I came in here like this, but it's very important.'

Dr Ndeti stood up. 'Who are you? What . . .' he began.

But Teresa hurried on. 'Please listen,' she said. 'You see, I know a secret medicine. It can prevent river blindness. Rose, this medicine woman, told me. She lives in the forest near Lake Victoria and all the young people in her village can see. She uses the leaves of a special tree. But Dr McCall wants to sell the secret to F.D.I. He wants the million dollars. He doesn't want to help Village International . . .'

Teresa heard a laugh behind her. She knew that laugh. She turned quickly and looked towards the window. Dr McCall was sitting there and smiling at her.

'Dr McCall! But . . .' Teresa's eyes were wide with surprise. 'But . . . you left me alone in the camp. You gave me tea that made me sick . . . I told you the secret. You're . . . You're . . .' Teresa's eyes were aching again, and her head was going round and round. She didn't understand anything. There were noises in her ears.

'You're making a terrible mistake, young woman,' said Dr Ndeti angrily. 'Dr McCall has told us – Village International – about the medicine. He has been working all his life for the people of Kenya.'

Dr McCall smiled sadly. 'Teresa, come here,' he said.

She went slowly towards him.

'Look into my eyes.'

Teresa felt afraid. 'He *is* a strange man,' she thought. 'What shall I do?' She looked at Dr Ndeti.

'Yes, look into his eyes,' he said.

Teresa went nearer to the doctor. He took off his dark glasses and opened his eyes wide. They were red and tired. Like Rose's eyes . . . Rose's eyes! But Rose was going blind . . .

'Do you need a microscope?' the doctor asked quietly. 'A

million dollars won't help me much, will it?'

'Oh no! I didn't know . . . I'm sorry, I'm sorry . . .' Teresa's head went round and round, and suddenly everything went black.

◐ ◐ ◑ ◑

A few days later Teresa and Christopher were having lunch together in a restaurant.

'What happened that day, when I fainted in Dr Ndeti's office?' asked Teresa.

'Oh, it was very exciting,' smiled Christopher. 'People were shouting and talking. Dr Ndeti was saying, "Who *is* this girl?" He wanted to call the police. And Dr McCall was helping you, and saying, "Poor girl, poor girl, she's got heatstroke." I thought you were sick when you came to my office, but you didn't want to listen to me.'

'No,' said Teresa. 'I didn't know I had heatstroke. I was in Dr McCall's hospital for three days. He was very kind to me.' She looked down at her plate. 'I felt very silly. I didn't know about his eyes. I didn't like him because he didn't help at the camp, and he shouted at me. I thought he didn't want to help anybody. I was afraid of him, and when he gave me that tea, and I felt so sick, I thought . . . But I was wrong. He knew I had heatstroke. I was wrong about everything.'

'But why did he suddenly go to Nairobi and leave you alone?' Christopher asked.

'He left me a letter. He wanted to fly to Nairobi immediately with the good news for Village International. He wanted them to get the money from Norway. He loves Kenya and the Kenyans and wants to help them as much as possible. He didn't want the money from F.D.I.' Teresa smiled. 'He left the letter in my bag, but I didn't see it. He told Obediah to come back and look after me. But when Obediah got back to the camp, I wasn't there! I feel terrible about it.'

'Why didn't he tell you everything earlier?' said Christopher.

'He didn't trust me. He thought I was too young . . . and a bit silly. Maybe I was . . .'

'Don't worry, Teresa.' Christopher smiled. 'Dr McCall isn't angry with you now, is he?'

'No, he thinks it's funny! I don't know why. But I never want to see Dr Ndeti again. He was very angry with me.'

'Oh, Teresa! Well, Village International will help all the people with that medicine now. They'll get the money from Norway and every child in Kenya will have the medicine. Be happy!'

'I am. Oh, I am.'

'What are you going to do now?' Christopher looked at Teresa. 'Are you going back to England? Or do you want to learn more about Africa?'

'Oh yes! I love it here. I love the space, the sky, the flowers, the birds.' She laughed happily. 'In the mornings I'm going to help Dr McCall in his hospital . . . and you could give me a job as a reporter! I'm good at writing stories.'

'You're certainly good at inventing them!' smiled Christopher. 'Let's drink to that.' And they lifted their cups of coffee.

Exercises

1 Read through the story quickly and find this information.

1 The time Teresa will stay in Kenya.
2 Dr McCall's nationality.
3 The African language that Anna Holmes speaks.
4 Teresa's age when she left Kenya.
5 Teresa's age in the story.
6 Christopher Mwale's job.
7 The country that promised Village International a lot of money.
8 The number of dollars that Village International will get.
9 The drink Dr McCall gave Teresa when she came back to the camp.
10 The number of days Teresa was in hospital.

2 Are these sentences true (√) or false (×)?

1 Teresa knew Kenya well.
2 Dr McCall could not speak Nandi.
3 There were no roads to Rose's village.
4 Rose did not want to tell Dr McCall the secret.
5 Rose wanted the million dollars for herself.
6 Teresa returned to the camp alone.
7 Teresa was ill when she told Dr McCall the secret.
8 Rose's medicine for river blindness was made from a flower.
9 Dr McCall sold the secret of the medicine to F.D.I.
10 Village International will be able to give the medicine to every child in Kenya.

3 Comprehension questions

1 Why was Teresa going to Kenya?
2 Why could Teresa speak Nandi?
3 How do people catch river blindness?
4 What work do the blind people in the villages do?
5 What did Dr McCall want Teresa to do for him?
6 Why didn't Dr McCall want to use a Kenyan?
7 Why was Christopher Mwale interested in Dr McCall?

8   Why did Teresa think Dr McCall wanted to sell the medicine to F.D.I.?
9   Why was Teresa angry with Dr McCall at the camp?
10 What did Teresa take with her for the walk to Rose's village?
11 Why was Rose surprised when Teresa spoke to her?
12 Why didn't Rose want to tell Dr McCall about the flower?
13 How many times did Dr McCall visit Rose?
14 How did Rose make the medicine?
15 Why was Christopher Mwale excited when Teresa came to his office?
16 What was the matter with Dr McCall's eyes?
17 Why did Teresa faint in Dr Ndeti's office?
18 Why did Dr McCall go back to Nairobi?
19 Why was Dr Ndeti angry with Teresa?
20 What did Teresa want to do at the end of the story?

4 Complete the spaces in these sentences.

1   'You must drink a lot of water here, or you'll become . . . .'
2   'It attacks the eyes and, very slowly, the person goes . . . .'
3   'When someone has river blindness, no doctor can . . . . . it.'
4   'Now, remember, it's a . . . . Don't talk to anyone about it.'
5   Many people believe there will soon be a . . . . . for river blindness.
6   'I think he wants to get the . . . . . dollars for himself.'
7   'Ask her to show you the flower that . . . . . river blindness.'
8   'I will not tell him. I do not . . . . . him. I will tell you. Only you.'
9   'You're making a terrible . . . . . , young woman.'
10 'He thought I was too young, and a bit . . . . . . Maybe I was.'

5 Discussion questions

1   Describe the life of the blind people in African villages.
2   Describe the walk through the forest to Rose's village.
3   Describe Teresa's heatstroke. Why did she get heatstroke?
4   Was Dr McCall a good man or a bad man? How do you know?
5   Do you think Teresa was 'too young, and a bit silly'?
    Why?/Why not? How did she feel at the end of the story?
    Do you think she learnt anything?

Glossary

blind (go blind): unable to see; become unable to see
blindness: doctors can sometimes cure blindness and make people see again
boil: make water, etc, very hot; you boil water when you make tea
breathe: take air into your lungs through your nose or mouth and send it out again
bundle: a number of things that are tied together
camp: a place where people live in tents or huts for a short time
catch (an illness): get an illness or a disease
charity: an organization (not a business company) that helps people, e.g. blind people, poor people, hungry people, etc
cure: make someone's illness better
director: the most important person in a company or an organization
disease: something that makes people ill or sick
drug: a medicine or chemical that can make sick people well
faint: become unconscious ('asleep') for a short time because of an illness, too much hot sun, etc
fly: a small insect (a kind of animal) with wings that flies
heatstroke: an illness; too much hot sun on the head can give people heatstroke
huge: very, very big
hut: a small building, often made of wood
invent: think of something, e.g. a story, that is not real or not true
lake: a large area of water with land all around it
leaf/leaves: small green part(s) of a tree or a plant
lion: a wild animal, the largest of the wild cats
medicine: something that can make sick people well
medicine woman: a woman in places like Africa who is not a doctor but who knows a lot about medicines from plants, etc
microscope: a scientific instrument; you put something very small under it and the microscope makes it look larger
prevent: stop something before it happens
sickness: an illness
silent: without any sound; not speaking
still: not moving

tent: a shelter (a small 'building') made of cloth, poles and ropes; people sleep in tents in camps

tiny: very, very small

trust: believe that a person or thing is good, true, strong, etc

worm: a small, thin animal without legs or arms that often lives in earth; it looks like a tiny snake